Salame & Signor

Text: Viveca Sundvall
Illustrations: Gunilla Wärnström

Published by Lundby of Sweden

I'm Tommy: Tommy Lund, 8 Orange Lane, Lundby, Sweden, Europe, the World, the Universe.

I'm six, but I've got eight freckles. My big sister, Linda, is actually eight but she doesn't have any freckles. She's crazy about horses and keeps going on all the time about having her own horse. It gets pretty boring having to listen to that . . .

Me, I like frogs.

There's a park near our house—so close by that I'm allowed to go there on my own. But I'm the only one who knows there's a pond there—a secret pond, with frogs!

I've caught four. First I had them in the washbasin in the bathroom, but then mother started screaming when she was going to wash her hair. Now they're in a tub on the balcony outside Linda's room. She doesn't know though, because I've covered the tub with a rug. The fact is Linda's a bit scared of frogs so it's best I keep things quiet. She probably thinks they're just ordinary old snakes in my tub. You'd like to know what my frog friends are called?

Well, they are Quack One, Quack Two, Quack Three and Quack Four—so now you know!

We've only lived in our house for a week. It's sort of exciting because sometimes I get lost. One morning when I woke up I was hungry so I ran off to the kitchen to have an egg and cornflakes—that's my favorite breakfast . . . And where did I finish up? In the wardrobe. That's how big our house is!

Before that we lived in an apartment in town and Linda and I shared a room. But now I have my own room, with a sloping ceiling! It's fun just to lie in bed and gaze up at the window in the roof, especially when it's raining. I have bunk beds in my room. Linda and I used to share them before.

I sleep on the top one and Tom-Tom has the one underneath. Tom-Tom is my puppy and I like him better than anyone else in the whole house. Tom-Tom likes to gnaw on shoes. And he also likes to run in the park with me and look for frogs. Tom-Tom is nice to frogs.

Linda has her own pets too, a couple of cats she calls Grey and White. But they never go with her to the park. Grey and White go where they want. Probably that's why Linda keeps going on about horses all the time.

What does our house look like?
Well, up on the roof there's a chimney.
Next time the chimney sweep comes I plan
to go on the roof with him and look down
inside the chimney. If Tom-Tom behaves
himself I'll let him come up too. Tom-Tom
and I live on the upstairs floor. It's great
having my own room, though I miss Linda
sometimes. When we shared a room she
told me super ghost stories—if she was in
the mood, of course . . .

Next to my room is the bathroom and be-
yond the bathroom is Linda's room. I'm a
bit envious of her because she has a little
balcony. Mother says she wouldn't sleep a
wink if I had a balcony outside my room.
She thinks I'd go sleepwalking and bal-
ance on the balcony rail—maybe she's
right about that! Below my room is the
kitchen and that suits me fine because I
can hear through the floor when they're
making pancakes down there. My dad
Martin, and my mother Mary, sleep in the
room next to the kitchen. We're not allowed to jump on their bed. Then there's
the living room where we eat when we
have visitors.

Now what have I forgotten? Oh, of course, I've forgotten grandma. She's called Ellen. They're working on grandma's apartment in town so she's staying with us for a few weeks—in Linda's room. Grandma brought her rocking chair with her when she came. She can't go anywhere without that!

I forgot grandma and I forgot the basement too. Down there we have a rumpus room with a TV and a log fireplace and weight-lifting stuff. There's a laundry room with an extra bed for visitors. The garage is next door. There's a car in there and a few bikes. When I grow up I'm going to have eight motorcycles.

There's something else too—Linda's special retreat. She calls it a stable and it does look a bit like a stable, except that there are no horses! The stable is full of old furniture, rugs, skates, a birdcage, a broken down sewing machine and a lot of old photograph albums. Linda likes to sit in there with all that junk and dream about her own horse. He would be brown and he'd be called Michael.

As far as I'm concerned, I think frogs are more fun.

Yesterday Quack Three got away!

This evening we're going to have a visitor and mother and grandma are cleaning up frantically. Dad's out in the kitchen making French fish soup. He learned how to do that when he lived in France one summer when he was young. It's pretty good soup really, but it's the only food he knows how to fix.

Our visitor is Mr Moll; the great Mr Moll! Me, I'm not looking forward to it at all. He doesn't have any children and no dog. I'm sure he doesn't know anything about frogs.

Mother has invited Mr Moll to stay with us because he was her first boss when she was young and worked in a bank in London. She worked every day then and stayed with Mr Moll and his wife. Now Mrs Moll is dead and Mr Moll is all alone. So he's coming to stay with us, live in the laundry room and eat fish soup.

— Maybe we should put up the flag, I suggested.

— Right, said dad, I'm glad you thought of that. What flag shall we put up, the Swedish one?

— Of course, I said, I mean, we do live in Sweden, don't we?

So now Mr Moll is here. He was really impressed when he saw the Swedish flag flying. He also liked the French fish soup. Afterwards we had a Christmas pudding from London, all burning with flames, so that he wouldn't get to feeling too homesick.

Mr Moll seemed very pleased to be with us and he brought a big plant in a pot for mother.

— What a charming man, murmured grandma as she watched Mr Moll. I've always had a weakness for grey moustaches and shiny shoes.

After supper Mr Moll played the piano for us. He played something called Stardust which is an old-fashioned bit and mother and grandma hummed along in tune and clapped afterwards.

— It's a fine, warm evening, said dad. Maybe we should have our coffee on the balcony.

— Not likely, said mother. And how are we going to get the piano upstairs on the balcony?

And right then Linda suddenly got the best idea ever . . .

— Look mother, said Linda, why don't Tommy and I sleep out on the balcony tonight?
— Never in your life, answered mother. You'll both catch colds and probably fall down in to the garden!
— Come on, dad, I said . . .
— No way, answered dad. There could be spiders and bats and rain and thunder . . .
Grandma looked up from her knitting:
— What an exciting idea; sleeping on the balcony. When we were kids we used to sleep out in the garden under the trees on warm nights like this. That kept us very healthy.

Mr Moll stopped playing the piano.
— When I was a lad we used to camp in a tent by the river, he said—by the Thames. It was supposed to be good for us.
Mother and dad gazed at grandma and Mr Moll. They looked healthy enough, both of them—so we were allowed to sleep on the balcony.

We rushed up and got our mattresses and pulled out our sleeping bags and fixed our beds on the balcony. Everything was just fine.

— What's under that rug, asked Linda, pointing to my frog tub.

— Nothing special, I said. Maybe it's just some tulip bulbs that mother's going to plant in the window boxes this fall. Linda suddenly whipped off the rug.

— F R O G S!!! she yelled.

— What's wrong with frogs, I asked. This is Quack One, Quack Two and Quack Four. Now say hullo to Aunt Linda, boys!

— Shut up! yelled Linda. Then she ran into her room and jumped on her bed.

— I'm sorry about that, I said to Quack One, Quack Two and Quack Four. My sister just doesn't understand frogs.

I carried the tub into the kitchen and put it on the draining board.

Linda and I then got into our sleeping bags on the balcony and shone our flashlights at each other. Linda told a terrifying ghost story about a princess with no head, but she fell asleep in the middle of it, and so did I.

All of a sudden I woke, listening to a strange sort of swishing sound. I sat wondering first if mother was down frying eggs maybe. But then I saw it was all dark everywhere so it couldn't possibly be breakfast time.

I heard the noise again, much louder—a terrific sort of swishing like the sound of huge birdwings.

The next instant a gigantic swan landed on the balcony railing. It was so big that the railing creaked.

Linda woke now as well, and sat up. We stared at each other and just as I was about to say something she signed me to keep quiet and pointed to the balcony door that was opening.

Out came grandma in her long blue and white-striped nightgown. She had her knitting in one hand and she walked straight over to the balcony railing without even noticing that Linda and I were awake.

— It's a good thing for you Margaret, she said speaking to the swan, that you finally found your way here. The swan looked a bit sullen.

— You can soon move back to your apartment in town. It is a lot nicer than this balcony, muttered the swan in reply.

— All right, all right, said grandma and then, hoisting up her nightgown, she climbed on the swan's back.

Linda and I gaped at each other and then shouted together:

— Grandma, we want to come too!

Grandma looked startled.

— Oh dearie me, she said. I'd forgotten that you two were sleeping out here on the balcony. Now you know my secret and I'm not sure that's a good thing. Get down in your sleeping bags again and forget all about what you've just seen and heard!

We sat still.

Margaret the swan glared at us.

— And who might these little characters be? she demanded.

— They're my grandchildren Linda and Tommy, said grandma proudly. Just look how big they're growing.

— To me they look about as big as field mice, replied the swan.

— Then it won't make any difference if we come along too, said Linda quickly. Where are you going?

— We're going to Frog Isle, said grandma, and sighed. I'm the night porter there. I'm the one who looks after Margaret.

— Looks after her? . . . whispered Linda.

— Yes, I make grass soup for her and clean up her home, and brush her wings . . .

— And makes me eat horrid vitamins, added the swan miserably.

— We promise we won't say a word to a soul, said Linda and I together.

Grandma nodded, and we got on Margaret's back.

It was so fluffy and soft sitting on Margaret's back, but she was in a bad temper nevertheless. When we flew over the park I leaned a bit to one side to see if there were any nice frogs in the pond and Margaret began at once to complain:
— Sit straight up there, she shrilled. How can I steer properly with you behaving like that?
— Do as Margaret says, pleaded grandma, otherwise she'll get into an even worse mood and complain about the food I fix for her.
— But why do you go flying around on Margaret at nights and work at that island? we asked.

— Well, replied grandma, we all have to have some sort of hobby when we're retired. Some people collect stamps, others sing in the church choir. Me, I take care of an ill-tempered swan every full moon.
— But how did all this begin? asked Linda.
— I found her sitting on my balcony one evening, said grandma. It was just a matter of climbing on her back, that's all.
— Keep quiet up there, shouted Margaret. You're deafening me with your chatter!

The air felt much cooler when we flew out over the sea.

— Shouldn't we be wearing life preservers? asked Linda, terrified. She didn't dare look down. But I did. The water looked all black while over our heads the stars glittered and the moon looked as big and round as cheese.

— We will soon be there now, said grandma.

In the middle of the dark ocean we could see a green spot which got larger and larger the closer we came to it.

— Is that Frog Isle? asked Linda. Why is it called Frog Isle? There aren't any frogs there, are there?

— Packed with 'em, answered grandma. Tame ones and wild ones.

I tingled with delight all the way down to my toes. Just imagine if I'd been able to take Quack One, Quack Two and Quack Four with me on this excursion.

— Hold on, we're coming in to land, called Margaret.

— What about putting down the under-carriage? I called back.

I knew what I was talking about because I'd flown in a plane once. Down to Majorca in Spain. That time the pilot had been very careful to put the wheels down before landing.

— Now don't upset Margaret, whispered grandma, and in an instant we came down with a soft bump in the middle of the green island.

— Welcome to Frog Isle, said grandma cheerfully. Do as you wish now and we'll meet again just when the moon goes down. Stay out of the castle with cobwebs on the roof.

— But grandma, said Linda, aren't you going to look after us?

— Look after you? Ha! cried grandma and her eyes looking greener than usual. She put her knitting under a stone and undid her hair bun. I'd never seen her like that before. Her hair reached all the way down to her knees.

— No, she said, you two must look after yourselves. It's Margaret that I have to look after. But don't forget to be right here by this stone when you can no longer see the full moon in the sky.

— Come on now Ellen and stop babbling, hissed Margaret and made off into the green woods.

And there we stood . . .

— I'm scared, I said to Linda.

— Not me, answered Linda. It seems to smell like horses from that path over there. Come on, let's have a look.

— I'd rather go looking for frogs, I muttered.

I felt a bit miserable somehow.

Linda wandered cheerfully down the long path. Once she smells a horse then she's not afraid of anything.

I ran after her and she took my hand. Sometimes she's very nice to me.

It was pretty walking along this path and not dark at all because the moon was shining. On the ground you could see hoof marks, but there was no sign of a horse. Suddenly the path curved away very sharply.

We stood still in our tracks.

— Do you see what I see? whispered Linda and pointed.

— You bet I do, I answered. Whoever saw frogs like that!

Sitting on a white bench were the two biggest frogs I'd ever seen in my life. One was wearing a straw hat and the other had a black top hat, the sort of thing granddad wears when he's going somewhere very formal.

— Frogs fiddlesticks, said Linda. What I meant was that castle!

There at the end of the path was the most beautiful castle. Just like the ones in fairy story books.

— No big deal, I said, that's just an old castle. Take a look at those frogs instead.

— Quite so, said the frogs, very pleased with themselves.

They could talk our language too.

— I'm Signor, said one of the frogs. Now that we were standing in front of them I could see that Signor was wearing some medals, that were real gold! I knew that because my granddad had a medal made of gold in his desk drawer. He had won it in a dancing competition when he was young.

— Real gold! I said.

Signor looked very pleased indeed.

— I'm Salame, said the other frog.

— What's that? replied Linda, not very politely.

In fact it was rather difficult to hear what Salame said because he was eating sausages all the time. He had a whole long string of them and there were still at least eight left.

— Care for a sausage? he asked.

— No thanks, we answered. We just don't have time for eating right now.

— Oh dear, said Signor sadly. Don't talk about eating because then I'm reminded of something awful.

— Now don't talk about that, said Salame. What are your names?

— We're called Linda and Tommy, answered Linda.

— Is that so? said Signor. Now which of you is Linda and which of you is Tommy?

— What's that beautiful castle? asked Linda.

— That, replied, Salame, is Princess Gabriella's castle. It's a pretty dull place really. She does nothing but try on dresses day in and day out. She's got a whole ice-box full of sausages and cucumbers and melons yet all she does is gaze at herself in the mirror.

— Is she a real princess? asked Linda. I didn't think there were any real ones. Does she have a crown on her head?

— Oh yes, sometimes, yawned Signor. But one thing she doesn't have is any medals.

— Are there cobwebs on the roof of the castle, asked Linda, because our grandma has told us not to go inside if there are!

— No, silly, said Salame. There are two castles on Frog Isle. The other one's full of snakes, beetles and cockroaches. That's where Princess Pamela lives, and that's where the cobwebs are.

Suddenly the two frogs began to tremble.

— We're scared of Princess Pamela, said Signor. She's never eaten frog legs and now we've heard she wants to try some.

— Well, said Linda, cheekily, I'm quite certain she would not want to eat frog legs as fat as yours. Come on Tommy, let's go in the castle.

And off we went.

The ceilings were high in the castle rooms and the floors were so polished you could have gone skating on them. Unfortunately I didn't have any skates with me. On one wall there was a huge mirror and there in front of it Princess Gabriella stood gazing at herself.

We knew at once, of course, that it was Gabriella, because next to her hung a whole row of dresses.

— Now does this pink really suit me? she sighed, turning this way and that before the mirror. Doesn't the pale blue dress with lace round the hem suit me better?

— No, I don't think so, replied Linda. I think you're very pretty in that.

— Well how sweet, said Gabriella and she tripped over and kissed Linda on the cheek. It's very important that I'm the most beautiful of all, because very shortly Larry and Arthur are coming here for a party.

Sounds fun with some other kids, I thought to myself, I just hope they know how to kick a ball around.

— Arthur and Larry are big princes, explained Gabriella. Arthur has blond hair and has just won the competition as the most handsome prince in Europe. Larry is dark and very good with addition, subtraction and all that. Well now, I think I'll try on my yellow dress.

— Hold it, I said, hold it a moment. I've worn my jeans every day since April and they're just about the sharpest things I have.

Linda stamped hard on my toe.

So I decided to go out to talk to the frogs instead, but Linda couldn't tear herself away from Gabriella's frocks. It was just as well for Gabriella, I thought, that she was bigger than Linda, otherwise Linda would have started trying on her clothes too.

I was very disappointed when I got outside, the frog bench was empty. There wasn't a sign of Salame or Signor. Just as I was about to go back into the castle again I heard someone coming. It was a big, very splendid peacock that marched out onto the gravel in front of the castle, with all its beautiful tail feathers spread.

This peacock looked every bit as pleased with itself as Margaret in fact. Then it caught sight of me and stopped.

— Who are you? I asked. By this time I had come to understand that all the animals on Frog Isle could talk.

— I'm Fine Florence, isn't that obvious? croaked the peacock. In fact I'm First Peacock at the Court of Princess Pamela. First and Finest . . .

— Is that so, I said, and just how many peacocks does she have there?

— One, of course, croaked Florence. And now I'm looking for two fat frogs that Princess Pamela wants for her dinner. Have you by any chance seen a couple of frogs around with very plump legs?

— No, no I haven't, I replied. The only frogs I've seen had very skinny legs—like matchsticks.

Fine Florence marched away without another word and I ran back inside to look for Linda.

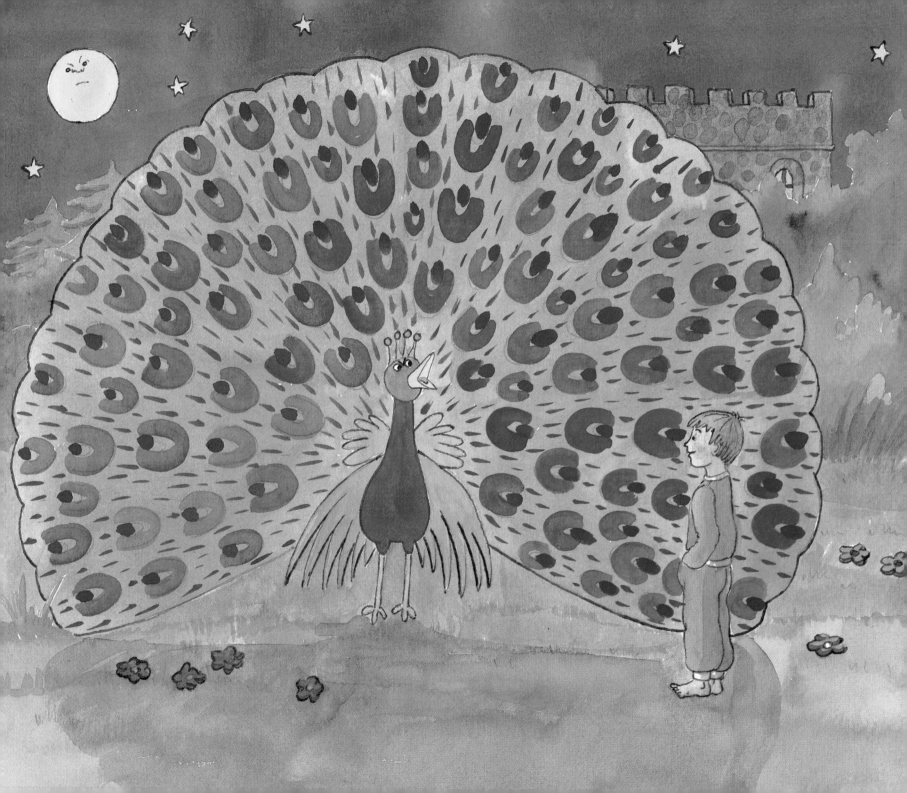

— We have to rescue Salame and Signor, I gasped. Princess Pamela is planning to eat them up!

— How absolutely awful, exclaimed Linda.

— It's worse than awful, it's perilous, muttered a voice from behind a gooseberry bush. Linda and I ran round the back of the bush and there sat Salame and Signor, trembling with fear.

— Once Florence finds us, that's it, groaned Signor. Ours are the plumpest frog legs on the whole island.

— I shall soon eat my last sausage, whimpered Salame.

— No, I said patting them both on the shoulder. I'm going to save you, you'll see . . .

Linda wasn't about to pat the frogs, but she did look at them in a friendly way.

— What we have to do, said Linda firmly, is get along to Cobweb Castle and talk some sense into that princess' head.

— But Linda, I said, you know grandma told us not to go into any castle that had cobwebs on the roof!

— But it was you who said this was a matter of life and death, replied Linda gravely.

— How do we go about getting there? I asked.

— Well, how about that, for instance, said Linda, and pointed at a pink motorcycle that was propped up against the castle wall.

Salame and Signor each hopped into a saddlebag and I climbed on the seat behind Linda. She had already started the bike and off we went.

— Funny that you should be able to drive a motorcycle, I shouted.

— Funnier still that the exhaust smells like a horse, she shouted back.

And it really did smell like a horse. I looked down into the saddlebags.

Signor had taken off his top hat and was polishing his medals with a little checkered handkerchief. Salame sat in the other bag chewing on a sausage.

— Now you must keep quiet so that you're not discovered in there, I said and patted them on the shoulder again, first Signor then Salame.

I know just how to handle frogs.

Salame and Signor nodded in agreement. We reached Cobweb Castle in no time at all. It looked terrible. The same turrets and towers as on the other castle but there were nasty looking bats hanging from the windows and the roof was covered in cobwebs. Florence strutted up and down before the doorway, scratching in the gravel.

— Just take care of this, will you, said Linda, and handed the motorcycle over to her. It needs washing off and more gas . . .

The walls of Princess Pamela's castle were covered in moss and the princess herself sat playing weird music on a harp. I had to get hold of Linda's hand again and I suddenly wished I were back home. It sounded nicer somehow, listening to Mr Moll playing Stardust than this eerie harp stuff. But Linda went bravely up to the princess and shouted in her ear:

— Are you Pamela?

The princess stopped playing.

— Where did you two midgets turn up from? she demanded, pointing at us with long black nails. You look as if you came out of a dolls house!

— We might not be very big, said I, but we're not stupid either. We don't eat frog legs for instance.

— Is that so, said Pamela. What do you eat then, raisins?

— As a matter of fact we do, I said, and we eat pizzas, popcorn, hamburgers, codfish, crabs, shrimps, parsley . . .

— And soda pop, added Linda.

— I've had all those things thousands of times, said Pamela, not to mention rattlesnake, octopus, snails, crocodile, jelly babies and crowmeat. But now I'm tired of all that and I want to try frog legs. They say they taste great. Grilled frog legs with fried onions. I've sent Florence out to find some nicely fattened frog legs.

How could we ever save Salame and
Signor?
We gazed around. In Cobweb Castle there
were no mirrors on the walls but there
were plenty of moose antlers, bear heads,
crocodile skins, rhinoceros horns and dried
elephant ears.
— We've been over at Gabriella's, announced Linda. She's going to have a party
tonight and you're invited too.
— Course I am, replied Pamela, she's my
sister. What sort of silly thing is she going
to wear this time?

— A pink dress with tulle I think, answered Linda. What are you going to wear?
— I think I'll put on my lizardskin over-
alls. I dance really well in those. Arthur
and Larry just love to dance with me.
The two of us thought furiously.
— Would you like a cup of snake-tea?
asked Pamela.
— Oh yes please, answered Linda quickly.
While Pamela was out in the kitchen
brewing the tea Linda whispered to me
that she had an idea. Just as she had fin-
ished explaining this Pamela came back
with three cups of green snake-tea.

We sipped the tea. It wasn't too bad really.
— Secret recipe, whispered Pamela. Rattle-snake and vinegar are the main ingredients. The rest I can't tell you. But it's very satisfying isn't it? And that's just as well I guess, because I don't suppose we'll get anything worth eating at Gabriella's. I've simply got to have a couple of nice plump frog legs so I'll have the strength to dance.
— I suppose you know, said Linda, that you can't dance when you've eaten frog legs.
— What do you mean, said Pamela. Of course I can!

— Not until three days afterwards, insisted Linda. A person who eats frog legs can't dance for the next three days. All he can do during that time is hop lika a frog.
— Well that's awful, gasped Pamela. Neither Arthur nor Larry would like it if I hopped about like a frog when they wanted to dance and hold me close . . . You're not kidding me are you?
— My little brother here could tell you about when our granddad was supposed to take part in a dancing competition, said Linda.

— Our granddad is always very active, I said. He just loves dancing, for instance. Well, he was going to take part in one of those big dance competitions; jitterbug, tango and waltz and all that.

— Yes, yes, said Pamela very interested. Go on, go on . . .

— The competition was being held in Paris and granddad and the others in our team went there by airplane.

— Never mind the details, said Pamela. Get on with what happened.

— Well, they were in a restaurant up in the Eifel Tower and they all ordered onion soup, except granddad who asked for frog legs. When he got them he thought they tasted good. But that evening the big dance competition started at the Olympia and there were lots and lots of people there to watch.

The first part was the jitterbug and granddad won that right way. He lept about like a frog and they all thought that was how people danced the jitterbug where he came from. So he got a gold medal for that. But then he was supposed to dance a tango and he went on leaping about like a frog, and it was even worse when it got to be time for the waltz. The audience all stood up and whistled and booed and in the end granddad had to pack up and go home. In fact he could hardly get on the plane because he was still frog-hopping when he went up the gangway. He stayed like that for ages afterwards. But he has always been extra nice to frogs since then!

Pamela shuddered.

— I've never heard anything so awful, she said and then she yelled:

— FLORENCE!

The door opened and pleased-with-herself Florence pranced in, picking her way through the moss and dust on the floor.

I've decided, announced Pamela, never to eat frog. So you can stop looking for frogs, I think instead I'll have some blueberry pie before I go to Gabriella's dance. And while you're at it you might as well put up a sign saying that all frogs on the island are to be protected by law and may not be harmed by anyone.

— Why not? asked Florence sulkily. I loathe frogs.

— Don't you understand me, said Pamela impatiently. I don't want anyone else to eat frogs in the future either.

— Just imagine if Arthur and Larry suddenly started hopping about like frogs. I wouldn't like that at all.

As Princess Pamela said this there was an odd noise from somewhere behind the harp and then Salame and Signor came cartwheeling out.

They rushed up to me and kissed me. Then they hugged and kissed Linda. She stood very still while they did this and tried not to shudder too much. And she smiled as best she could.

— And what about me? said Pamela. I've always dreamed of being kissed by a frog. Salame and Signor both politely removed their hats before kissing the princess on each cheek. She beamed with delight.

The full moon was still shining in the night sky when we came out of Cobweb Castle.

— That's fine, said Linda, because now we can go to Gabriella's party for a little while.

We got on the motorcycle that was newly polished and ready to go. Salame and Signor jumped quickly down into the saddlebags.

Pamela climbed on to Florence's back and they were off at once across the gravel.

— Drive carefully now, Pamela ordered Florence, otherwise next time I'll take a billy-goat taxi.

Salame pulled at my hand.

— How long are you two going to stay on the island? he asked.

— Only until the full moon goes behind the clouds, answered Linda sadly.

— That'll be soon, said Signor.

We drove silently through the woods and it seemed to me a bit sad somehow. I'd very much like to have taken Salame and Signor back home with me. I could have moved all the stuff out of my room into the stable and fixed up somewhere for them to live. Frogs, after all, are more important than furniture.

But I knew, of course, that they'd never really want to leave their island. I mean, they were protected by law now.

The castle was all lit up and looking love-ly.
Two horses were tethered outside, one brown and one white.
— They're the horses of Arthur and Larry, explained Signor. Arthur's a very hand-some prince.
— But Larry's very good at counting sau-sages, said Salame. He's best.
— I know what's best of all, cried Linda and, dropping the motorcycle, she ran over to the horses. Of course she had lump sugar and old apples in her pockets, she al-ways did—in case she met a horse some-where. And now she had found two!

I was allowed to go into the castle by my-self—with Salame and Signor of course . . . Inside the dance had already begun. Pame-la was dancing with Larry and Gabriella was dancing with Arthur. Florence danced with Margaret. Salame and Signor started hopping around together until their hats tumbled off.
The dance music was terrifically loud, but it didn't matter too much because there weren't any neighbors around. Then sud-denly I began to feel a bit weary so I sat down on a sofa and nibbled on some sau-sages that Salame had hidden under the cushion. I wondered to myself as I sat there if I would ever be able to teach Quack One and Quack Two and Quack Four to talk . . .

Suddenly the castle door flew open and Linda called to me:
— Hurry up Tommy. I can scarcely see the moon anymore. We've got to run to grandma and the stone!
We said goodbye to Gabriella first, because it was her party.
— Come again another time, she said. Then you can bring me some flowers.
— Oh, now don't pay any attention to my sister, said Pamela, she's only kidding. But you could bring me a few choice cockroaches from your country. It's been a long time since I last tasted a really juicy cockroach.

Larry came up, too, to say goodbye. Linda ran forward and kissed him on the forehead and he looked very surprised.
— I just wanted to see if you would change into a frog, said Linda. My brother and I are just crazy about frogs.
— Is it true that you really have mini-calculators in your country, mumbled Larry. I can't see the point of it myself. Listen: 378 times 291 is 109,988. It's simple . . .
—Get up on my back and sit properly, ordered Margaret.
We did so and the next moment she flew straight out through the window.

Grandma was sitting on the stone knitting. She had done her hair up in a bun again.

— Oh, so you found each other, she said when Margaret landed and she scrambled up behind us on the swan's back. What have you been up to all this time?

— Nothing special, we answered.

— Just so long as you haven't been in Cobweb Castle, said grandma.

We didn't say anything.

— Oh, so you have, have you, said grandma. Well, well, we all have our little secrets. I must take a nap now so I'll be alert at breakfast tomorrow. I wonder what Mr Moll usually has for breakfast?

— Two fried eggs and cornflakes, I suggested.

— Banana and cucumber, suggested Linda.

— Oh—I don't know. Grandma wasn't really satisfied. It ought to be something more exotic, so that Mr Moll sort of feels that he's at a party all day long. Russian caviar maybe—no that's too expensive. Oysters, oysters are good. No—now I know—fried frog legs, that's what I'll get him!

— No, no, yelled Linda, that's not allowed. All frogs are protected by law!

When Margaret landed on the balcony rail it was already getting light. Linda and I were so exhausted that we simply fell into our sleeping bags and went straight to sleep.

I woke up to hear a clinking sound. It was mother bringing us orange juice and buns.

— Are you two going to sleep all day? she asked. Dad's already jogged two miles round the park and now he's weightlifting. Mr Moll and grandma are having breakfast in the kitchen and you two are still lying here snoring . . .

— What are they having? I cried.

— I don't know, answered mother, some funny looking stuff, green, that Mr Moll brought with him.

I rushed down into the kitchen.

— What are you eating? I demanded.

— Spinach cereal from Liverpool and sour milk, said grandma smiling.

I dashed back up to Linda again who was still sitting in her sleeping bag rubbing her eyes.

— I had the funniest dream last night, she said.

— So did I, I said.

She put her hand in the pocket of her pyjamas.

— My apples have gone, she said, and so have my lumps of sugar. And look at this:

In her hand she held a little medal and a sausage.

I felt in my pocket and, sure enough, there, too, was a little medal and a sausage. Strange, wasn't it?

Something was wriggling around inside my sleeping bag. Quack Three had come back again. I gave him the sausage—and the medal.

He looked very pleased with himself.